THE MELLOW FELLOW
WHO PLAYED THE CELLO

BY ZACK VARRATO

To Mom, Dad, and every teacher nurturing a
world where all birds can flock together

This feathery fellow was always mellow.
He played his cello wherever he went.
His mind was open to all people and places,
So the Mellow Fellow's days were happily spent!

GO AWAY

But the bird next door was a different story.
"Grumpy Grouch" was the name he earned over time.
He kept to himself and never went out
As if making friends were some sort of crime!

"Won't you come out of your house, Mr. Neighbor?"
The Mellow Fellow asked him one day.
"I'll show you the world and some reasons to smile.
It's not as bad out there as you say!"

The Grouch grumbled and groveled and tried to stay put,
But the Mellow Fellow dragged him out.
The cello had played only a few notes more before
The Grouch found something to complain about!

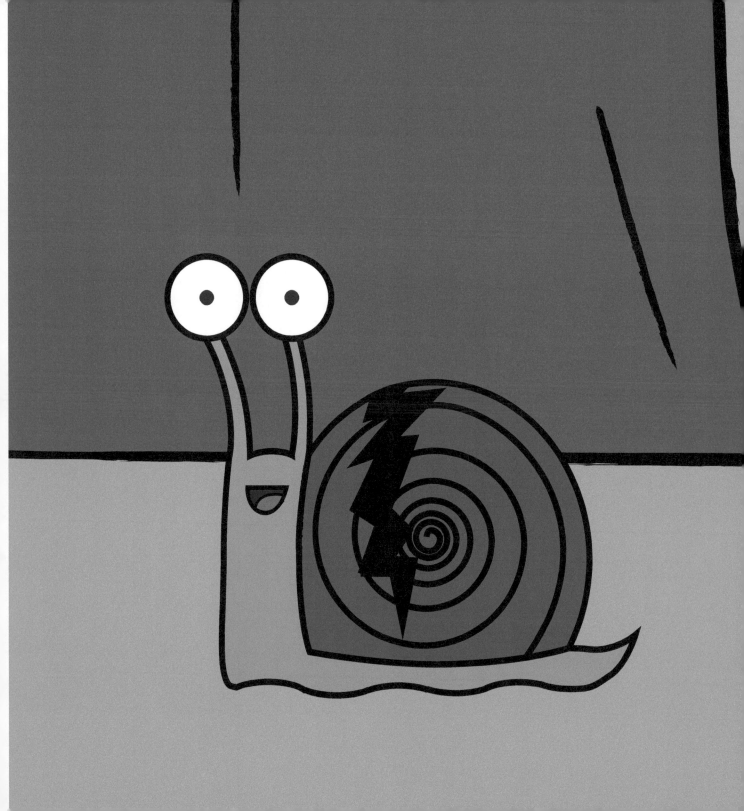

"Just look at that snail! That can't be normal.
He was born with a crack, and such a slow pace!"
The Mellow Fellow still played his cello and said,
"Mr. Snail is kind, and THAT wins the race."

"Someone PURPLE moved in next door.
Surely that makes you feel under the weather."
But the Mellow Fellow still played his cello and said,
"Our town is open to ALL colors of feather!"

When they flew to the town, the Grouch was so grumpy!
"They're holding wings, those two boy canaries."
But the Mellow Fellow still played his cello and said,
"The canaries can marry who they want to marry!"

When they reached the town, the Grouch saw a penguin.
"Don't you wish he'd go back where he's from?"
But the Mellow Fellow still played his cello and said,
"We don't own this town. Anyone can come!"

"Oh, how strange those rabbits look!" the Grouch exclaimed.
"Look at the hats and the turbans they wear!"
But the Mellow Fellow still played his cello and said,
"No matter the religion, there are many beliefs we share!"

"And if you're surprised by the people so close to home,
Just wait till you see the wonders beyond!
With all the world's countries and cultures and climates,
I'm sure we'll find something of which you are fond!"

But the Grumpy Grouch did not like the South Pole.
He complained, "This place is nothing but ice!"
The Mellow Fellow still played his cello
because he thought the cold weather was nice!

The Grumpy Grouch did not like the Sahara Desert.
He said he simply could not stand the heat!
But the Mellow Fellow still played his cello.
He thought the sand felt good on his feet!

The Grumpy Grouch did not like the Pacific Ocean.
He did not want to be friends with the scaly creatures.
But the Mellow Fellow still played his cello.
He did not mind their sharp, white features!

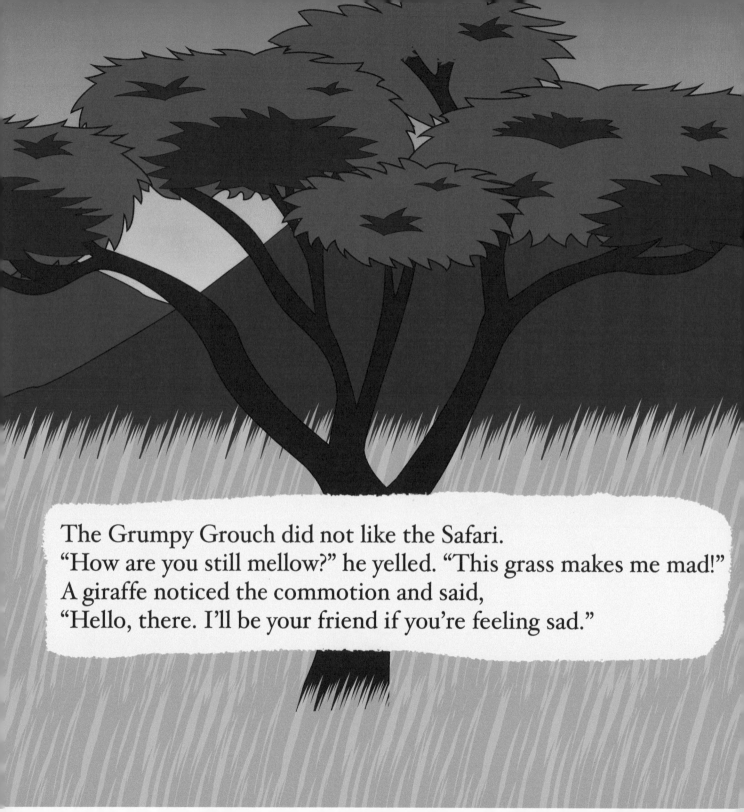

The Grumpy Grouch did not like the Safari.
"How are you still mellow?" he yelled. "This grass makes me mad!"
A giraffe noticed the commotion and said,
"Hello, there. I'll be your friend if you're feeling sad."

The Grumpy Grouch stomped on the ground and shouted,
"Well, YOU sure need friends. That much is true!
But with your long, spotted neck and high-pitched voice,
Who on Earth would be friends with you?"

The Mellow Fellow STOPPED playing his cello.
The Mellow Fellow was
NO
LONGER
MELLOW!

"There is ONE thing that upsets me!"
    the Mellow Fellow exclaimed.
"Not this giraffe, his voice, or the looks of his neck.
What bothers me is BULLYING:
Treating someone like an unworthy speck!"

Life would be no fun at all
If we all looked and acted the same.
You should be glad we are all very unique.
Our differences are not reasons for shame!

If you want to be happy and not quite so grumpy,
Go out in the world and make a new friend.
Accept all types of people from all types of places
And soon your grouchiness will end!

The Grumpy Grouch apologized for bullying the giraffe
And the giraffe expressed his gratitude.
After discovering what upset the Mellow Fellow,
The Grumpy Grouch changed his attitude!

"I'm sorry.
I'll be your friend, too!"

ABOUT THE AUTHOR / ILLUSTRATOR

Zack Varrato grew up in a small town of many feathers in southern Delaware. Raised by an elementary school librarian and a high school English teacher/author, he began writing and illustrating stories from a young age, and drafted early versions of the Mellow Fellow in high school. He graduated from the University of Pennsylvania, and now lives in Boston. Connect with him at www.ZackVarrato.com.

CPSIA information can be obtained
at www.ICGtesting.com
Printed in the USA
LVHW072103230721
693549LV00003B/42